Miss Read
Village Christmas.

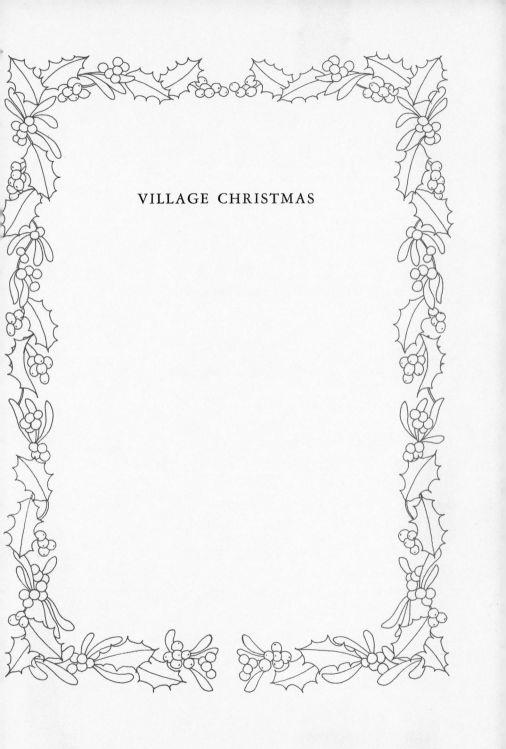

VILLAGE CHRISTMAS

ALSO BY MISS READ

Village School

Village Diary

Storm in the Village

Thrush Green

Fresh from the Country

Winter in Thrush Green

Miss Clare Remembers

Over the Gate

Saint, Doris Jessie.

VILLAGE CHRISTMAS

Miss Read, pseud.

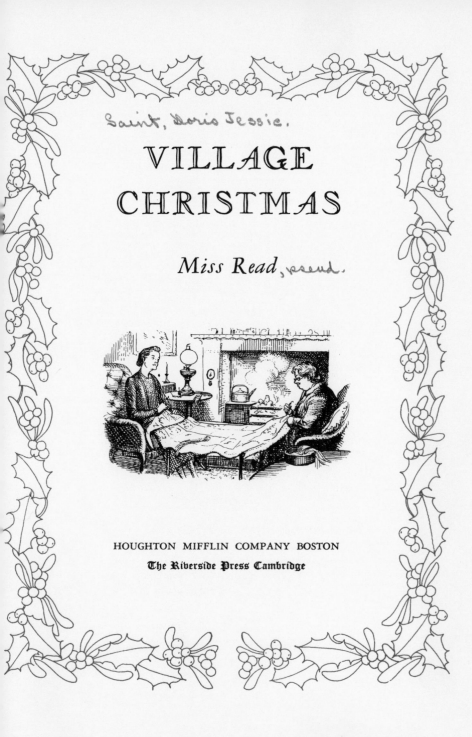

HOUGHTON MIFFLIN COMPANY BOSTON

𝕿𝖍𝖊 𝕽𝖎𝖛𝖊𝖗𝖘𝖎𝖉𝖊 𝕻𝖗𝖊𝖘𝖘 𝕮𝖆𝖒𝖇𝖗𝖎𝖉𝖌𝖊

Y

Title-page and endpaper illustrations
by J. S. GOODALL

Third Printing   w

Library of Congress Catalog Card Number: 66-19843
Printed in the United States of America

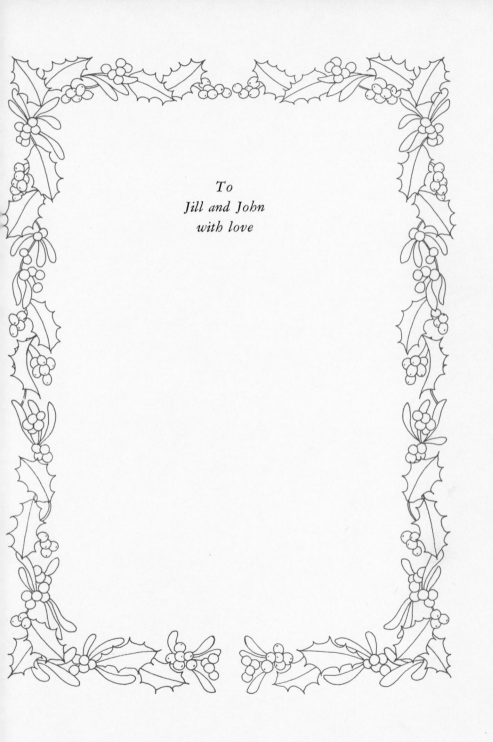

To
Jill and John
with love

VILLAGE CHRISTMAS

THE DARKNESS throbbed with the clamor of church bells. The six sonorous voices of St. Patrick's peal chased each other, now in regular rhythm, now in staccato clashes, as the bellringers sweated at their Christmas peal practice.

The night was iron-cold. Frost glittered on the hedges and fields of Fairacre although it was not yet eight o'clock. Thatched roofs were furred with white rime beneath a sky brilliant with stars. Smoke rose in unwavering blue wisps from cottage chimneys, for the air was uncannily still.

The sound of the bells carried far in such weather. At Beech Green, three miles away, Miss Clare heard them clearly as she stooped to put her empty milk bottle tidily on her cottage doorstep, and she smiled at the cheerful sound. She knew at least four of those six bellringers, for she had taught them their early lessons long ago at Fairacre school. Arthur Coggs, furtively setting rabbit snares in a copse near Spring-bourne, heard them as clearly. The shepherd high on the downs above the village and the lonely signal-man tending his oil lamps on the branch line which meandered along the Cax valley to the market town, heard them too.

Nearer at hand, in the village of Fairacre, the bells caused more positive reactions. The rooks, roosting in the topmost boughs of the elm trees hard by the reverberating belfry, squawked an occasional protest at this disturbance. A fox, slinking towards Mr. Willet's hen run, thought better of it as the bells rang out, and beat a retreat to the woods. Mrs. Pringle, the dour cleaner of Fairacre school, picked up a flake of whitewash with disgust from the spotless floor where it had fluttered from the quaking kitchen wall, and a new baby nearby, woken by the clamor, wailed its alarm.

Miss Margaret Waters and her sister Mary were quietly at work in their cottage in the village street. They sat, one at each side of the big round table in the living room, penning their Christmas cards in meticulous copperplate. Music tinkled from the large old-fashioned wireless set on the dresser by the fireplace, vying with the noise of the bells outside. Mary's gray curls began to nod in time to a waltz, and putting her pen between her teeth, she rose to increase the volume of the music. At that moment an excruciating clashing of St. Patrick's peal informed the world of Fairacre that at least three of the six bellringers were hopelessly awry in their order.

"Switch it off, Mary, do! Them dratted bells drowns anything else. We may as well save the electric!" exclaimed Margaret, looking over the top of her gold-rimmed spectacles.

Mary obeyed, as she always did, and returned to her seat. It would have been nice, she thought privately, to hear "The Merry Widow Waltz" all the way through, but it was not worth upsetting Margaret — especially with Christmas so near. After all, it was the season of good will. She picked up a card from the central pile and surveyed it with affection.

"All right for Uncle Toby?" she queried, her head on one side. "He's partial to a robin."

Her sister looked up from her writing and studied the card earnestly. Sending just the right card to the right person was something which both sisters considered with the utmost care. Their Christmas cards had been chosen from the most modestly priced counter at Bell's, the Caxley stationer's, but even so the amount had been a considerable sum from the weekly pension of the two elderly sisters.

"You don't feel it's a mite spangly? That glitter on the icicles don't look exactly *manly* to me. I'd say the coach and horses myself."

Mary set aside the robin reluctantly, and began to inscribe the card with the coach and horses:

From your affectionate nieces,
Margaret and Mary

The ancient mahogany clock, set foursquare in the middle of the mantelpiece, ticked steadily as it had done throughout their parents' married life and their own single ones. A log hissed on the small open fire, and the black kettle on the trivet began to hum. By bedtime it would be boiling, ready for the sisters' hot-water bottles. It was very peaceful and warm in the cottage and Mary sighed with content as she tucked in the flap of Uncle Toby's envelope. It was the time of day she loved best, when the work was done, the curtains were drawn, and she and Margaret sat snugly and companionably by the fire.

"That seems to be the lot," she observed, putting the envelopes into a neat stack. Margaret added her last one. Three, including the rejected robin, remained unused.

"There's bound to be someone we've forgot," said Margaret. "Put 'em all on the dresser, dear, and we'll post 'em off tomorrow."

The church bells stopped abruptly and the room

4

seemed very quiet. Ponderously and melodiously the old clock chimed half-past eight from the mantelpiece, and Mary began to yawn. At that moment there came a sharp rapping at the door. Mary's mouth closed with a snap.

"Who on earth can that be, at this time of night?" she whispered. Her blue eyes were round with alarm. Margaret, made of sterner stuff, strode to the door and flung it open. There, blinking in the sudden light, stood a little girl.

"Come in, do, out of the cold," begged Mary, who had followed her sister. "Why, Vanessa, you haven't got a coat on! You must be starved with the cold! Come by the fire now!"

The child advanced toward the blaze, plump hands outstretched like pink starfish. She sniffed cheerfully and beamed up at the two sisters who looked down at her with so much concern. The child's two front milk teeth had recently vanished and the gap gave her wide smile a gamin air. She shook the silky fringe from her sparkling eyes. Clearly, Miss Vanessa Emery was very happy to be inside Flint Cottage.

"And what do you want, my dear, so late in the day?" inquired Margaret, unusually gentle.

"Mummy sent me," explained the child. "She said

5

could you lend her some string to tie up Grandpa's
parcel. *Thick* string, she said, if you could manage
it. It's a box of apples, you see, off our tree, and sticky
tape won't be strong enough on its own."

"Indeed it won't," agreed Mary, opening the dresser
drawer and taking out a square tin. She opened it
and placed it on the table for the child to inspect.
Inside were neat coils of string, the thickest at the
left-hand side, and the finest — some of it as thin as
thread — in a tidy row on the right-hand. The child
drew in her breath with delight and put a finger
among the coils.

"Where did you buy it?" she asked.

"*Buy* it?" echoed Margaret, flabbergasted. "Buy
string? We've never bought a bit of string in all our
borns! This comes off all the parcels that have come
here over the years."

"Mum cuts ours off and throws it away," explained
the child, unabashed. She picked up a fat gingery coil
of hairy twine and examined it closely.

"Could you spare this?" she asked politely.

"Of course, of course," said Mary, hurrying to make
amends for the horrified outburst from her sister. She
tucked it into the pocket on the front of the child's
cotton apron.

"And now I'll see you across the road," she added, opening the front door. "It's so late I expect you should be in bed."

The child left the fire reluctantly. One hand gripped the string inside her pocket. The other she held out to Margaret.

"Goodnight, Miss Waters," she said carefully, "and thank you for the string."

"You're welcome," replied Margaret, shaking the cold hand. "Mind the road now."

The two sisters watched the child run across to the cottage opposite. It sat well back from the village street in a little hollow, surrounded by an overgrown garden. Against the night sky its thatched roof and two chimneys gave it the air of a great cat crouched comfortably on its haunches. They heard the gate bang, and turned again to their fire, slamming the door against the bitter cold.

"Well!" exploded Margaret. "Fancy sending a child out at this time of night! And for a bit of string! 'Cuts it off' indeed! Did you ever hear of such wicked waste, Mary?"

"Dreadful!" agreed her sister, but with less vehemence. "And that poor little mite with no coat on!"

"Well, I've always said, there's some people as have no business to be parents and them Emerys belong to 'em. Three under seven and another on the way! It's far too many. I feel downright sorry for that poor unborn. She can't look after the three she's got already!"

Margaret picked up the poker and rapped smartly at a large lump of coal. It split obediently and burst into joyous flame. The kettle purred with increased vigor, and Margaret moved it further back on the trivet.

The two sisters sat down, one at each side of the blaze. From the cupboard under the dresser Mary drew forth a large bundle, unrolled it, and gave one end to Margaret. They were making a hearth rug, a gigantic monster of Turkish design, in crimson and deep blue. Each evening the sisters spent some time thrusting their shining hooks in and out of the canvas as they laboriously added strand after strand of bright wool.

Margaret's end was growing much more quickly than Mary's. Her hook moved more briskly, with sharp staccato jabs, and the wool was tugged fiercely into place. Mary moved more slowly, and she fingered each knotted strand as though she loved it. She

8

would be sorry when the work was finished. Margaret would be glad.

"I must say, they seem happy enough," observed Mary, reverting to the topic of the Emerys. "And very healthy too. They're dear little girls — and so polite. Did you notice the way Vanessa shook hands?"

"It's not the children I'm criticizing," replied Margaret. "It's their parents. There'll be four little mites under that roof soon, and dear knows how many more to come. And they don't seem to have any idea of bringing them up right! Look at their fancy names, for one thing! Vanessa, Francesca, Anna-Louise — I ask you!"

"I rather like them," said Mary with spirit. Margaret snorted and jabbed the canvas energetically.

"And all dressed up in a frilly little apron with a heart-shaped pocket, and no decent warm coat on the child's back," continued Margaret, now in full spate. "It's all on a par with the house. All fancy lamp shades, and knickknacks hanging on the wall, and great holes in the sheets, for all to see, when she hangs 'em on the line. 'Twasn't no surprise to me to hear she cuts up her string and throws it out. We done right, Mary, not to get too familiar with her. She's the sort as would be in here, everlasting borrowing, given half a chance, as I told you at the outset."

"I daresay you're right, dear," responded Mary equably. She usually was, thought Mary, pensively. They worked in silence and Mary looked back to the time when the Emerys had first arrived in Fairacre, three months before, and from a vantage point behind the bedroom curtain she had watched their furniture being carried up the brick path.

***

It was a golden afternoon in late September and Margaret had gone to St. Patrick's to help with the decorations for Harvest Festival. A bilious headache had kept Mary from accompanying her, and she had retired to bed with an aspirin and a cup of tea.

She had slept for an hour and the sound of children's voices woke her. At first she thought the schoolchildren must be running home, but it was only three o'clock by the flowered china timepiece on the mantelshelf, and she had gone to the window to investigate.

A dark green pantechnicon almost blocked the village street. The men were staggering to the house opposite with a large and shabby sideboard between them. Two little girls danced excitedly beside them, piping shrilly to each other like demented moorhens. Their mother, cigarette in mouth, watched the proceedings from the side of the doorway.

Mary was a little shocked — not by the cigarette, although she felt smoking was not only a wicked waste of money but also very unhealthy — but at the young woman's attire. She wore black tights, with a good-sized hole in the left leg, and a short scarlet jerkin which ended at mid-thigh. Her black hair was long and straight, and her eyes were heavily made up. To Mary she appeared like an actress about to take part in a play set in the Middle Ages. No one — absolutely no one — dressed like that in Fairacre, and Mary only hoped that the young woman would not hear the remarks which must inevitably come from such village stalwarts as Mrs. Pringle and her own sister if she continued to dress in this manner.

Nevertheless, Mary was glad to see that they had neighbors, and gladder still to see that there were children. The thatched cottage had stood empty all the summer, ever since the old couple who had lived there from the time of their marriage in good Queen Victoria's reign had departed to a daughter's house in Caxley and had moved from thence to Fairacre churchyard. It would be good to see a light winking through the darkness again from the cottage window, and to see the neglected garden put into order once more, thought Mary.

Her headache had gone and she straightened the bed coverlet and made her way down the steep dark staircase. She was pleasantly excited by the activity outside the front door, and tried to hear what the children were saying, but in vain. A thin wailing could be heard and, peeping out from behind the curtain, Mary saw that the woman now had a baby slung over her shoulder and was patting its back vigorously.

"Three!" breathed Mary, with delight. She was devoted to children and thoroughly enjoyed taking her Sunday School class. To be sure, she was often put out when some of the bigger boys were impudent, and she was quite incapable of disciplining them, but small children, and particularly little girls of gentle upbringing, delighted her warm old spinster's heart.

When Margaret returned she told her the good news. Her sister received it with some reserve.

"I'll be as pleased as you are," she assured Mary, "if they behaves themselves. But let's pray they ain't the squalling sort. You can hear too much in that bedroom of ours when the wind's that way."

"I wondered," began Mary timidly, "if it would be a kindness to ask 'em over for a cup of tea when we makes it."

"If she was alone," replied Margaret after a moment's consideration, "I'd say 'Yes,' but with three children and the removal men too, I reckons we'd be overdone. Best leave it, Mary — but it does you credit to have thought of it."

Mary was about to answer, but Margaret went on. Her expression was cautious.

"We don't want to be too welcoming yet awhile, my dear. Let's see how they turn out. Being neighborly's one thing, but living in each other's pockets is another. Let 'em get settled and then we'll call. Best not to go too fast or we'll find ourselves baby-sitting every evening."

A thought struck her.

"Seen the man, Mary?"

Mary admitted that she had not.

"Funny!" ruminated her sister. 'You'd have thought he'd be on hand."

"Maybe he's clearing things up the other end," suggested Mary.

"Maybe," agreed Margaret. "I only hope and pray she's not a widow woman, or worse still one that's *been left.*"

"We'll soon know," replied Mary comfortably, well versed in village ways. Fairacre had a lively grapevine, and there would be no secrets hidden in the cottage opposite, the sisters felt quite sure.

✳✳✳

Within a week it was common knowledge that the Emerys had moved from a north London suburb — Enfield, according to Mrs. Pringle, Southgate, by Mr. Willet's reckoning, though the vicar was positive that it was Barnet. Much to Margaret's relief, Mr. Emery had appeared, and her first glimpse of him was as he put out the milk bottles the next morning whilst still clad in dashing crimson pajamas with yellow frogging.

He worked "up the Atomic," as did many other Fairacre residents, but drove there in a shabby old Daimler about nine, instead of going on the bus which collected the other workers at seven-thirty each morning.

"One of the high-ups," commented Mr. Willet. "Had a bit of book-learning in science and that, I don't doubt. Looks scruffy enough to have a degree,

to my mind. Wants a new razor blade, by the looks
of things, and that duffle coat has seen a few meals
down it."

Fairacre was inclined to agree with Mr. Willet's
somewhat tart summing-up of Mr. Emery, though the
female residents pointed out that he seemed to take
his share of looking after the children and, say what
you like, he had very attractive thick black hair. It
was Mrs. Emery who provided more fodder for gossip.

As Mary had foreseen, her Bohemian garments
scandalized the older generation. And then, she was
so breathtakingly friendly! She had introduced herself to Mr. Lamb in the post office, and to two vener-
able residents who were collecting their pensions,
shaking hands with them warmly and asking such
personal questions as where they lived and what were
their names.

"Wonder she didn't ask us how old we be," said
one to the other when they escaped into the open air.
"She be a baggage, I'll lay. I'll take good care to steer
clear of that 'un."

She hailed everyone she met with equal heartiness,
and struck horror into every conservative Fairacre
heart by announcing her decision to join every possible
club and society in the village "to get to know people,"

15

and her intention of taking the little girls with her if the times of the meetings proved suitable.

"Terribly important for them to make friends," she told customers and assistants in the village shop one morning. Her wide warm smile embraced them all. She seemed unaware of a certain frostiness in the air as she made her purchases, and bade them all goodbye, with considerable gusto, when she left.

Margaret and Mary viewed their ebullient neighbor with some alarm. Three days after her arrival, when Margaret was already planning the best time to call, Mrs. Emery knocked briefly on the sisters' front door and almost immediately opened it herself.

"Anyone at home?" she chirped blithely. "Can I come in?"

Before the startled sisters could reply, she was in the room, with two beaming little girls following her.

"I'm your new neighbor, as I expect you know," she said, smiling disarmingly. "Diana Emery. This is Vanessa, and this one Francesca. Say 'Hello,' darlings."

"Hello! Hello!" piped the two children.

Mary collected her wits with remarkable composure. She found the Emery family attractive, despite their forward ways.

"There now!" she began kindly. "We were wondering when to call and see you. Won't you take a cup of coffee? Margaret and I usually have some about this time."

"I'll get it," said Margaret swiftly, glad to escape for a moment to take stock of the situation. Mary could see from her expression that she was not pleased by the invasion.

"Lovely!" sighed Mrs. Emery, flinging off a loose jacket of jade green, and settling in Margaret's armchair. The two little girls collapsed cross-legged on the hearth rug and gazed about them with squirrel-bright eyes beneath their silky fringes.

"What about the baby?" asked Mary, concerned lest it should have been left outside. The morning was chilly.

"Not due until the New Year," replied Mrs. Emery nonchalantly. "And jolly glad I shall be when it's arrived."

There was a gasp from the doorway as Margaret bore in the tray. She was pink, and obviously put out. Mary hastened to explain.

"I meant the *third* little girl," she said.

"Oh, Anna-Louise! She's fast asleep in the pram. Quite safe, I can assure you."

"We want a brother next time," announced Vanessa, eying the plate of biscuits.

"Three girlth ith three too many," announced Francesca. "Thatth's what my daddy thayth."

"That's a joke," explained Vanessa.

"Sometimes I wonder," their mother said, but her tone was cheerful.

Margaret poured coffee and tried to avert her eyes from Mrs. Emery's striped frock which gaped widely at the waist fastening, displaying an extraordinary undergarment of scarlet silk. Could it *possibly* be a petticoat, Margaret wondered? Were there really petticoats in existence of such a remarkable color?

Mary did her best to make small talk. It was quite apparent that Margaret was suffering from shock, and was of little help.

"Is there anything you want to know about the village? Perhaps you go to church sometimes? The services are at ten-thirty and six-thirty."

"We're not much good at churchgoing," admitted their neighbor. "Though I must say the vicar looks a perfect poppet."

Margaret swallowed a mouthful of coffee too quickly and coughed noisily. This was downright sacrilege.

"Gone down the wrong way," explained Francesca, coming close to Margaret and gazing up anxiously into her scarlet face. Speechless, but touched by the child's solicitude, Margaret nodded her agreement.

"And if you want to go to Caxley," continued Mary, "there is a bus timetable on the wall of 'The Beetle and Wedge.' Is there anything else we can help you with?"

Mrs. Emery put her cup carelessly upon its saucer so that the spoon crashed to the floor. Both children pounced upon it and returned it to the table.

"Well, yes, there is something," said their mother. "Could you possibly change a check for me? I'm absolutely out of money and want to get some cigarettes. Edgar won't be home until eight or after."

There was a chilly silence. The sisters had no banking account, and the idea of lending money, even to their nearest and dearest, was against their principles. To be asked, by a stranger, to advance money was profoundly shocking. Margaret found her tongue suddenly.

"I'm afraid we can't oblige. We keep very little in the house. I suggest that you ask Mr. Lamb. He may be able to help." Her tone was glacial, but Mrs. Emery appeared unperturbed.

19

"Ah well," she said cheerfully, struggling from the armchair and gaping even more hugely at the waistband, "never mind! I'll try Mr. Lamb, as you suggest. Must have a cigarette now and again with this brood to look after."

She picked up the green jacket and smiled warmly upon the sisters.

"Thank you so much for the delicious coffee. Do pop over and see us whenever you like. We'll probably be seeing quite a bit of each other as we're such close neighbors."

And with these ominous words she had made her departure.

※※※

Ever since then, thought Mary, busily prodding her hook in the rug, she and Margaret had fought a polite, but quietly desperate, battle against invasion.

"Be friendly to all, but familiar with few," said an old Victorian sampler hanging on their cottage wall. The sisters found its advice timely. The children, they agreed, were adorable, and although they appeared far too often for "a-shilling-for-the-electricity-meter" or "a-box-of-matches-because-the-shop's-shut" and other like errands, the two sisters had not the heart to be annoyed with them. In any case, it was simple to dismiss them when their business was done, with a piece of chocolate to sweeten their departure.

Mrs. Emery, growing weekly more bulky, was more difficult to manage, and the two sisters grew adept at making excuses. Once inside, she was apt to stay over an hour, seriously throwing out the working of the sisters' day. She certainly was an embarrassment as a neighbor.

Mary's eyes strayed to the table, and the rejected Christmas card with the gay robin among his spangles. A thought struck her, and she put down her hook.

"Margaret," she said suddenly, "what about sending that robin to the Emery children?"

Margaret began to look doubtful.

"Well, my dear, you know what a mite of trouble we've had with that woman! I just wonder — "

"Oh, do now!" pressed Mary, her face flushed. " 'Tis Christmas! No time for hard thoughts, sister, and them children would just love it. I could slip over with it after dark on Christmas Eve and pop it through the letter box."

Margaret's face relaxed into a smile.

"We'll do it, Mary, that we will!"

She began to roll up the rug briskly, as the church clock struck ten. Mary gave a happy sigh, and lifted the singing kettle from the trivet.

"Time for bed," she said, taking two hot-water bottles from the bottom of the dresser cupboard. "Think of it, Margaret! Only three more days until Christmas!"

❊❊❊

The next three days were busy ones for the ladies at Flint Cottage. Red-berried holly, pale mistletoe, and glossy ivy were collected and used to decorate the living room. Two red candles stood one at each end of the mantlepiece, and a holly garland hung from the brass knocker on the front door.

The cake was iced, the pudding fetched down from the top shelf in the pantry, the mincemeat jar stood ready for the pies, and a trifle was made. One of Mrs. Pringle's chickens arrived ready for the table, and sausage meat came from the butcher.

Margaret crept away privately while Mary was bringing in logs from the woodshed, and wrapped up two pairs of sensible lisle stockings which she had bought in Caxley for her sister's present. Mary took advantage of Margaret's absence at the post office and

22

swiftly wrapped up a pair of stout leather gloves and hid them in the second drawer of the bedroom chest.

All Fairacre was abustle. Margaret and Mary helped to set up the Christmas crib in the chancel of St. Patrick's church. The figures of Joseph, Mary and the Child, the shepherds, and the wise men reappeared every year, standing in the straw provided by Mr. Roberts, the farmer, and lit with somber beauty by discreetly placed electric lights. The children came in on their way from school to see this perennial scene, and never tired of looking.

The sisters helped to decorate the church too. There were Christmas roses on the altar, their pearly beauty set off by sprigs of dark yew amidst the gleaming silverware.

On Christmas Eve the carol singers set out on their annual pilgrimage round the village. Mr. Annett, the choir master, was in charge of the church choir and any other willing chorister who volunteered to join the party. This year, the newcomer Mr. Emery was among them, for word had soon gone round that he sang well and Mr. Annett had invited him to join the carol singers. Clad in the duffle coat which Mr. Willet thought of so poorly, he strode cheerfully along the frosty lanes of Fairacre, swinging a hurricane lamp as though he had lived in the village all his life, and rattling away to his companions with the same friendly foreign loquacity as his wife's.

One of their stopping places was outside "The Beetle and Wedge," strategically placed in the village street. Margaret and Mary opened their window and watched the singers at their work. Their breath rose in silver clouds in the light of the lanterns. The white music sheets fluttered in the icy wind which spoke of future snow to the weather-wise of Fairacre. Some of the lamps were hung on tall stout ash sticks, and these swayed above the ruffled hair of the men and the hooded heads of the women.

Mr. Annett conducted vigorously and the singing was controlled as well as robust. As country voices caroled the eternal story of joyous birth, Mary felt that she had never been so happy. Across the road she could see the upstairs light in the bedroom of the Emery children, and against the glowing pane were silhouetted two dark heads.

How excited they must be, thought Mary! The stockings would be hanging limply over the bed rail, just as her own and Margaret's used to hang so many years ago. There was nothing to touch the exquisite anticipation of Christmas Eve.

"Hark the herald angels sing,
Glory to the newborn King,"

fluted the choir boys, their eyes on Mr. Annett, their mouths like dark O's in the lamp light. And the sound of their singing rose like incense to the thousands of stars above.

※※※

On Christmas morning Margaret and Mary were up early and went to eight o'clock service. A feeling of night still hung about the quiet village, although the sun was staining the eastern sky and giving promise of a fine day ahead.

The lighted crib glowed in the shadowy chancel like the star of Bethlehem itself, and the aromatic smell of the evergreens added to the spirit of Christmas. Later, the bells would ring out and the winter sunshine would touch the flowers and silver on the altar with brightness. All would be glory and rejoicing, but there was something particularly lovely and holy about these quiet early morning devotions, and the two sisters preferred to attend then, knowing that the rest of the morning would be taken up with the cheerful ritual of Christmas Day cooking.

25

They unwrapped their few parcels after breakfast, exclaiming with genuine pleasure at the modest calendars and handkerchiefs, the unaccustomed luxury of richly perfumed soap or chocolates which friends and relatives had sent.

Margaret thanked Mary warmly for the gloves. Mary was equally delighted with her stockings. They exchanged rare kisses and told each other how lucky they were.

"There's not many," said Margaret, "as can say they live as contented as we do here. And under our own roof, thank God, and nothing owing to any man!"

"We've a lot to be thankful for," agreed Mary, folding up the bright wrappings neatly. "Best of all, each other — and next best, our health and strength, sister."

"Now I'm off to stuff the bird," announced Margaret, rising with energy. "I'll put on the pudding too while I'm in the kitchen. Must have that properly hotted up by midday."

She bustled off and Mary began to make up the fire and sweep the hearth. The two red candles looked brave and gay, standing like sentinels on each side of the Christmas cards ranged along the mantelpiece. She wondered if the Emery children had liked the fat robin. She could see them now, in imagination, surrounded by new Christmas presents, flushed and excited at the joy of receiving and of giving.

At that moment a rapping came at the front door and she rose from her sweeping to open it. Vanessa stood there, looking far from flushed and excited. The child's eyes were large with alarm, her face pale with cold and fright.

"What is it, my love? Come in quickly," cried Mary.

"It's Mummy. She said could you come over, please. She's ill."

"Is Daddy with her?" asked Margaret, appearing in the doorway with her fingers pink and sticky with sausage meat.

"No. He's had to go to Grandma's. Grandpa rang up last night after we'd gone to bed. Grandma's being stroked."

"Had a stroke," corrected Margaret automatically. "Dear me, that's bad news! We'll be over as soon as we've put the dinner in."

The child's eyes grew more enormous than ever. She looked imploringly at Mary.

"But it's the baby coming! You must come this minute. Please, please!"

Without a word Margaret began to take off her kitchen apron.

"Go over, Mary," she said quietly. "I'll follow you."

※※※

Indescribable chaos greeted Mary's eyes when she stepped into the Emerys' kitchen. It was a large square room with a brick floor, and comfortably warmed by an Esse cooker appallingly streaked with grime. Quantities of anthracite dust were plentifully sprinkled on the floor at its base, and had been liberally trodden about the room.

The debris of breakfast littered the table, and colored paper, tags, and string garnished sticky cereal bowls and mugs. A ginger cat lapped up some milk which dripped from an overturned jug, and the confusion was made more acute by Francesca, who stood proudly holding a new scarlet scooter, ringing the shiny bell without cessation.

"Give over, do!" begged Mary, peremptory in her flurry. The child obeyed, still beaming. Nothing could quench her Christmas bliss, and Mary was immediately glad to see that this was so. The sound of Anna-Louise's wailing became apparent, and Mary opened the door of the box staircase and began to

28

mount. The two little girls started to follow her.

"You stop here, there's dears," said Mary, much agitated. Who knows what terrors might be aloft? "Pick up the paper and make it nice and tidy."

To her relief they fell upon the muddle joyously, and she creaked her way above. Mrs. Emery's voice greeted her. She sounded as boisterous as ever, and Mary's fears grew less. At least she was conscious!

"You are a darling! You really are!" cried Mrs. Emery. She was standing by the window, a vast figure in a red satin dressing gown embroidered on the back with a fierce dragon. Mary suddenly realized how very young she looked, and her heart went out to her.

"We were so sorry to hear about your mother-in-law," began Mary, a little primly.

"Poor sweet," said Mrs. Emery. "It would have to happen now. Edgar went off as soon as he came back from carol singing. And then, this! *Much* too early. I suppose I've got the dates wrong again. Ah well!"

She sighed, and suddenly clutched the front of the dressing gown again. Mary felt panic rising.

"Do get into bed, there's a love," she begged, turning back the rumpled bed clothes invitingly. The bottom sheet had a tear in it six inches long, and a very dirty rag doll was also revealed. Poor Mary

29

was appalled. She must put something clean on the bed! Suppose the baby was born in that unhygienic spot! She looked for help towards Mrs. Emery, who was bowed before the chest of drawers and gasping in an alarming way.

"You must have clean sheets," announced Mary with an authoritative ring in her voice which wholly surprised her.

"Cupboard," gasped Mrs. Emery, nodding toward the next room.

An unpleasant smell was the first thing that Mary noticed about the adjoining bedroom. Anna-Louise was standing in a cot. Her nightgown and the bedding were ominously stained, but her cries had ceased and she threw Mary a ravishing smile.

"You pretty thing," cried Mary, quite entranced. "Aunt Mary'll see to you in just a minute."

She swiftly ransacked the cupboard. She found a roll of mackintosh sheeting and two clean linen ones. Bustling back to the bedroom she set about making the bed with vigorous speed. Mrs. Emery was upright again, leaning her damp forehead against the cool windowpane. She consented to be led to the bed, un-protesting, and let Mary remove the flamboyant dressing gown.

"There, there!" soothed Mary, tucking her in as though she were a child. "I'll bring you a drink."

"I'm all right now," whispered the girl, and at that moment Margaret appeared.

"Does Nurse know?" was her first remark. Mary felt suddenly guilty. Of course it was the first thing she should have found out. Trust Margaret to know exactly what to do!

"Yes," replied Mrs. Emery. "At least, someone at her house does. Nurse was out on another baby case. They were sending word."

"What about Doctor Martin?" continued Margaret.

"Nurse will get him, if need be," said the girl. She sank back on the pillow and suddenly looked deathly tired. "It won't come for hours," she told them. "It's just that I was worried about the children."

"I know, I know," said Margaret gently. "We'll look after them all right. Leave it all to us."

"Anna-Louise needs a wash," said Mary, retiring to the next room. She beckoned Margaret to follow her, and closed the door between the two rooms.

"What on earth shall we do?" she implored Margaret. Margaret, for once, looked flummoxed.

"Dear knows, and that's the honest truth," admitted her sister. "Let's hope nature knows best and Nurse comes pretty smartly. This is foreign stuff to us, Mary, but we must just hold the fort till help comes."

She turned to survey Anna-Louise, who was jumping rhythmically up and down in the cot with dire results.

"Land's sake, Mary! That child wants dumping in the bath — and the bedding too!"

"I'll do her," said Mary swiftly. "And then I can keep an eye on Mrs. Emery up here. You see to things downstairs."

"Won't do no harm to give Nurse another ring," observed Margaret, turning to the door. She looked back at her sister.

"Who'd 'a' thought we'd 'a' been spending Christmas like this?"

She vanished downstairs and Mary went to turn on the bath for her charge.

※※※

Anna-Louise, well soaped, was absolutely adorable. Fat and pink, with a skin like satin, she made Mary a willing slave. She patted the water vigorously, sending up showers of spray, and drenching Mary kneeling beside the bath. Mary could have stayed there all day, murmuring endearments and righting the celluloid duck time and time again. But the water cooled rapidly, and there was much to do. She gathered the naked child into a grubby bath towel, and dried her on her lap.

"She hasn't had her breakfast yet," Mrs. Emery said drowsily when the child was dressed. She looked at her daughter with amusement.

"That's Francesca's jumper," she observed, "but no matter. Tie a bib on the poor lamb. She's a filthy feeder."

Below stairs, all was amazingly quiet. The table had been cleared and the two little girls were blissfully engaged in filling in their new Christmas drawing books with glossy long crayons as yet unbroken. Margaret was busy sweeping the floor with a broom from which most of the bristles had long vanished.

"Has the baby come yet?" asked Vanessa, without looking up from the mad oscillation of her crayoning.

"Not yet," replied Mary, threading Anna-Louise's fat legs through her high chair. She stood back and surveyed the baby anxiously. "And what does Anna-Louise like for breakfast?"

33

Francesca put down her crayon and gazed earnestly at her younger sister.

"She liketh bacon rindth betht," she told Mary.

"Well, we've no time to cook bacon," said Margaret flatly, still wielding the broom.

"Egg," said Vanessa briefly. "All horrible and runny. That's what she likes."

The sisters exchanged questioning glances.

"Sounds reasonable," muttered Margaret, "if you can find the egg saucepan."

"It's the milk one as well," volunteered Vanessa, making for a cupboard. "Here you are." She produced a battered saucepan with a wobbly handle, and returned to the drawing book.

"Did you get through to Nurse?" asked Mary agitatedly, as she filled the saucepan.

"Still out. Message supposed to have been passed on. I reckons we ought to get her husband back. It's his business after all." Margaret spoke with some asperity.

"I'll go and ask Mrs. Emery," said Mary, "while the egg boils."

She returned to the bedroom to find Mrs. Emery humped under the bedclothes with her head in the pillow. She was groaning with such awful intensity

34

that Mary's first impulse was to fly for Margaret, but she controlled it. She patted the humped back consolingly and waited for the spasm to pass. Somewhere, far away it seemed, the bells of St. Patrick's began to peal for morning service. A vivid picture of the peaceful nave, the holly and the Christmas roses, the fragrance of the cypress and yew came clearly to Mary, standing helplessly there watching her neighbor in labor. How long ago, it seemed, since she and Margaret knelt in the church! Yet only three or four hours had gone by.

The spasm passed and Diana Emery's face appeared again.

"Better," she said. "Can I have that drink now? Coffee, please — no milk. Any sign of that confounded nurse?"

"She's on her way," said Mary. "And we thought we ought to phone your husband."

"His parents aren't on the telephone," said Mrs. Emery.

"We could ring the police," suggested Mary with sudden inspiration. Mrs. Emery laughed with such unaffected gaiety that Mary could hardly believe that she had so recently been in such pain.

"It's not *that* serious. Nurse will be along any

minute now, and think how wonderful it will be to present Edgar with a fine new baby!"

She sounded so matter-of-fact and cheerful that Mary gazed at her open-mouthed. Was childbearing really undertaken so lightly? She remembered Margaret's tart comments on people who had large families with such apparent fecklessness. How many more would there be in this casual household, Mary wondered? Then she remembered the sight of Anna-Louise in the bath and hoped suddenly, and irrationally, that there would be more — lots more — and that she would be able to enjoy them.

"I'll get your coffee, my love," she said warmly and went below.

Returning with the steaming black brew, she remembered something.

"Shouldn't we put the baby's things ready for nurse?" she asked.

"There's not a great deal," confessed the girl, warming her hands round the cup. "I intended to do most of the shopping after Christmas in Caxley. So many people about, I just couldn't face it."

"But you must have *some* things," persisted Mary, aghast.

"In the bottom drawer," said the girl vaguely. "And

there are lots of Anna-Louise's things that will do in the airing cupboard."

Mary was shocked at such a slapdash approach to an important event, and her face must have shown it for Mrs. Emery laughed.

"After the first you don't bother quite so much," she confessed. "You can get by with all the odds and ends the others had."

Mary found six new diapers in the drawer, and a bundle of small undershirts, some tiny nightgowns yellow with much washing, and a shawl or two in the airing cupboard.

"And what shall we put the baby in?" she inquired.

"Anna-Louise's carry-cot. It's in her room. It probably wants clean things in it." The girl had slipped down into the bed again and closed her eyes. She looked desperately tired, thought Mary, with a pang.

The carry-cot held two dolls, a headless teddy bear, and a shoe, all carefully tucked up in a checked table-cloth. Mary took the carry-cot downstairs to wash it out and dry it ready for the new occupant.

"If that dratted nurse don't come soon," said Margaret, "I'll fetch Doctor Martin myself, that

I will! I'll just slip over home, Mary, and turn that bird and add a mite of hot water to the pudding."

"We'll never have a chance to eat dinner, sister," cried Mary. "Not as things are!"

"There's them three to think of," replied Margaret, nodding at the children. "We've got them to feed, don't forget."

She lifted the latch and hurried across to their cottage, while Mary dried the carry-cot and took stock. One or two parishioners, in their Sunday best, were making their way to church. Mary saw Mr. and Mrs. Willet stop to speak to her sister as she stood with one hand on their doorknob. There was much head-shaking, and Mrs. Willet looked across at the Emerys' house with some alarm.

"The news will soon be round Fairacre," thought Mary, as she dried the carry-cot.

It was clean and peaceful now in the kitchen, and she noticed the paper chains festooned against the ceiling, and the Christmas cards pinned along the rafters. Her own fat robin was there, and she glowed with pleasure. Vanessa and Francesca were still engrossed in their artistic efforts, and Anna-Louise wiped her eggy plate with her fingers and sucked them happily. What dear good children they were, thought Mary!

At that moment she heard their mother calling from overhead. Her voice sounded shrill and desperate. Mary took the stairs at a run. The girl was sitting up in bed, clenching and unclenching her hands on the coverlet.

"You *must* get that nurse — or the doctor, or someone. I can't stick this now. It's coming pretty fast."

"I'll ring again," promised Mary, thoroughly frightened by the urgency of the girl's pleas. "Just lie down again. I'm sure it's better. Can I do anything? Rub your back, say, or bring you a hot-water bottle?"

She did her best to appear calm, but inwardly terror gripped her. Supposing the baby came this minute? What on earth did you do with a newborn baby? Wasn't there something about cutting a cord? And if so, where did you cut it? And how did you tie it up afterwards? Hadn't she heard once that mothers bled to death if the cord wasn't tied properly? And that wretched carry-cot wouldn't be anywhere near aired, let alone made up with clean bedding, if the baby arrived now! Mary found herself shaking with

39

panic, and praying desperately. Don't let it come yet, please, dear Lord! Not until Nurse arrives, please God!

"There, my love — " she began, when she stopped abruptly. The door of the staircase had opened and someone was mounting.

"Margaret!" she cried. "Quickly, Margaret!"

A sturdy figure appeared in the doorway.

"Nurse! Thank God!" cried Mary, and began to weep.

"You go and make us all a cup of tea," said Nurse Thomas with gruff kindness. And Mary fled.

※※※

An hour later, Margaret and Mary sat at their own table, serving three excited little girls with Christmas dinner. Nurse's car still stood outside the cottage opposite, but Doctor Martin's was not to be seen. Evidently all was going well, and Nurse had everything well in hand.

Mary found herself as excited as the children. What a relief it was to be at home again, and to know that Mrs. Emery was being properly nursed! It was impossible to eat amidst such momentous happenings, and she was glad to neglect her own plate and to have the pleasant task of guiding Anna-Louise's teaspoon in the right direction.

In the afternoon the youngest child slept soundly in Mary's own bed. St. Patrick's clock chimed three, and still no message came from the house across the road.

A few Fairacre folk began to go by, taking an afternoon stroll for the sake of their digestions between Christmas dinner and the further challenge of iced cake for tea. They noted Nurse's car and the light in the upstairs window, and fell to wondering.

Margaret was reading "The Tale of Two Bad Mice" from a new glossy copy which the children had received that morning when a tapping came at the door. Mrs. Lamb from the post office stood outside with a bouquet of anemones in her hand. She caught sight of the two little girls inside and spoke in a whisper.

"For their mother, my dear. Hope all's going well. We heard about it after church. You're going over again, I expect?"

"Yes, indeed," answered Margaret, accepting the bright bunch. "She'll be pleased with these. Nurse is still there, as you see."

She nodded toward the car.

"Give Mrs. Emery our best wishes," said Mrs. Lamb. "Poor soul, without her husband too! She's got everyone's sympathy, that's a fact."

She set off homeward, and Margaret returned to the fireside. It began to grow dark, for the afternoon was overcast, and Mary took a taper and lit the bright red candles. The flames stretched and dwindled in the draft and the little girls gazed at them starry-eyed.

"Do you always have candles?" asked Vanessa. "Or just at Christmas?"

"Just at Christmas," said Margaret.

She put down the book and gazed at the bright flames with the children. The waiting seemed endless, and suddenly she felt desperately tired. How much longer, she wondered, before they knew?

Just then they heard the sound of a gate shutting and footsteps coming to their door. Margaret and Mary exchanged swift glances. Could it be —?

Mary opened the door and there stood the nurse, smiling.

"Come in," said Mary.

"I daren't. I'm late now," said the nurse, "but all's well."

Margaret and the children gathered at the door.

"A boy," Nurse announced proudly. "Seven pounds and bonny. And Mrs. Emery's asleep. Can one of you go over?"

"You go," said Margaret to Mary. "I'll bring the children over later."

"We want to see him," pleaded Vanessa.

"*Now!*" added Francesca stubbornly.

"Now!" echoed Anna-Louise, not understanding the situation, but glad to try a new word.

"Later on," responded Nurse firmly. "Your mummy's tired."

She turned to go and then looked back.

"Mr. Emery rang up. I've told him the news and he'll be back very soon."

She waved and made her way across the road to the car.

"Tell Mrs. Emery I'll be in in the morning," she called, and drove off in a cloud of smoke.

As if by magic, two heads popped out from the doorway of "The Beetle and Wedge." They belonged to the landlord and his wife.

"Couldn't help seeing Nurse go off," he said to Mary. "What is it?"

"A boy," said Mary, smiling.

"Now, ain't that good news?" beamed his wife. "You tell her we'll be wetting the baby's head in here tonight."

"Ah, she's a grand little mother, for all her funny ways," declared her husband. "Tell her it'll be nice to have another young 'un in the village."

Mary tiptoed into the silent cottage. Everything seemed to slumber. The cat slept on a chair by the stove. Nothing moved.

She left the door of the staircase ajar so that she could hear the slightest sound from above, and sat down at the table.

In the domestic stillness which enveloped her, after the stress of the day, old and lovely words came into her mind. *And she brought forth her first-born son; and she wrapped him in swaddling clothes, and laid him in a manger . . .*

She slipped off her stout country shoes and tiptoed up the stairs. It was very quiet in the bedroom. Mrs. Emery, looking pathetically young and pale, slept deeply. Beside the bed, on two chairs, was the carry-cot.

Mary leant over and gazed in wonder. Swaddled tightly, in the shawl she had found for him in the airing cupboard, was the newborn baby, as oblivious

44

of the world about him as his sleeping mother. Full of joy she crept below once more.

There was a sound outside, and she looked up from lacing her shoes. There stood Mr. Emery, his face alight.

"Where is she?" he asked.

"They're both upstairs," whispered Mary, and opened the staircase door so that he could go aloft and see his son.

❋❋❋

Late that night, the two sisters sat at each side of the hearth, working at their rug.

"D'you know what Vanessa said when her father fetched her?" asked Margaret. "She said: 'This is the loveliest Christmas we've ever had!' 'Twas good of the child to say it, I thought, after such a muddling old day. It touched me very much."

"She spoke the truth," replied Mary slowly. "Not only for herself, but for all of us here in Fairacre. 'Tis a funny thing, sister, but when I crept up the stairs to take a first look at that new babe the thought came to me: 'Ah! You're a true Fairacre child, just as I was once, born here, and most likely to be bred up here, the Lord willing!' And then another thought

45

came: 'You've warmed up us cold old Fairacre folk quicker'n the sun melts frost.' You know, Margaret, them Emerys have put us all to shame, many a time, with their friendly ways, and been snubbed too, often as not. It took a Christmas baby to kindle some proper Christmas good will in Fairacre."

" 'Tis true," admitted Margaret, putting down the rug hook, and gazing into the dying fire. Into her tired mind there floated irrelevant memories . . . Mrs. Emery's scarlet petticoat, a ginger kitten lapping milk, Anna-Louise fumbling with her egg spoon while her sisters watched her with squirrel-bright eyes laughing at her antics . . . all adding up to color and warmth and gentle loving-kindness.

"Now this has happened," she said soberly, "it won't stop at *Christmas* good will, sister. The Emerys are part and parcel of this village for good. There's room for all sorts in Fairacre, Mary, but it took a newborn babe to show us."

She began to roll up the rug briskly.

"Come, sister. Time we was abed."